The Man With No Face

JOHN YEOMAN

Illustrated by David Kearney

WAYLAND

Chapter One

A few years ago my cousin Colin, who was two years older than me, used to bully me quite a bit. He's still two years older than me, but he doesn't bully me any more. In fact, he's always very nice to me now.

It all started way back, when we were both quite young. In the school holidays Colin would always spend a few days at our flat, and then I'd spend a few days at his.

Our flat is on the fifth floor of a new block. It's nice and sunny, but it's got low ceilings and feels a bit small. At that time Colin's flat was the ground floor of what my  mum calls a "Victorian" house. It had big marble fireplaces and tall ceilings with bumpy plaster decorations all round the edges. I thought it was a great place. Best of all I loved the cellar.

You went down into it through a door under the stairs. Although there was a light, a dim bulb with no shade, you had to pick your way carefully down the open wooden steps because they were partly in shadow and there was no handrail. That was the bit I didn't like.

It was a terrific place to play in if you couldn't play outside. Colin's parents had dumped a load of old stuff they weren't using down there. There were packing-cases, suitcases, hampers – things like that – and bits of unwanted furniture all over the place.

It was much untidier than my room ever is. And it smelled cool and sort of furry with dust, if you know what I mean.

At first I accepted being bossed about. After all, Colin was older than me and it was *his* cellar; and so it was only natural that he should be the leader.

If the packing-cases were a boat, he was always the captain and I was always scrubbing the decks. If we went on a polar expedition,

he always drove the sled
and I was the husky. If
the spaceship landed on
Mars, he was always the
commander and I was always the helpless
Martian he captured and tied up.

As though that wasn't enough to put
up with, as we got older he decided that
I wasn't putting enough
effort into the games.

"I don't want wimps in my team," he'd say, in the specially nasty voice he used when he was being mean. And that gave him the excuse for pinching me and punching me and hitting me across the backs of the legs with an old brass stair-rod.

"You deserve it," he'd hiss. "And it's no use whingeing to Mum and Dad. I'll only give you worse next time."

Chapter Two

One particularly wet and windy
afternoon in the Easter holiday Colin
suggested, which meant ordered, a game
of Cops and Robbers. Now I quite
enjoyed our version of Cops and
Robbers, which was like a cross between
Hide-and-Seek and Tag. The seeker
could easily set off in the right direction
and still take ages to spot the hider,

because there were so
many little alley-ways
to slink down and
corners to turn. Often
it was just a faint
shadow or a creaking
wicker basket or a

dusty sneeze that gave the hider away.

I was rather smart at it, or lucky, that
afternoon. I kept catching Colin, mostly
by standing still and waiting for him to
come face to face with me. That didn't
put him in a very good mood.

"Don't look so pleased with yourself," he snapped, giving my hair a hard tug. "The afternoon's not over yet. There's still plenty of time for me to get even."

I know that, whatever I was feeling, I wasn't *looking* pleased with myself. Experience had taught me that Colin always became resentful if I was clearly happy, and when Colin became resentful he turned vicious.

After we'd had some sandwiches and washed them down with thin orange squash, and Colin had belched a few times

(to remind me that there were certain things that he could do much better than I could), he announced that we were going to have round two of Cops and Robbers.

"You can hide first," he said, in a voice that sounded more like an order than a favour. It surprised me a bit as he always claimed that it was his turn, whether it was or not, but I wasn't going to argue. I had a good place behind an old bookcase in mind.

I must admit that I always found this part of the game a bit scary. In the eerie silence I'd find myself imagining that I could hear other sounds – like a rat scratching or bones being crunched.

I crouched behind that bookcase for ages, waiting for the faint tell-tale sound that would let me know in which direction Colin was moving. To pick up the real clues you had to hold your breath and train your heart to stop thumping. Straight ahead of me, on the dirty brick wall, the faint shadows looked like headstones in a graveyard.

It was much longer than usual before I caught the first tiny squeak of Colin's trainers, and then it seemed to come from an unexpected direction, near the foot of the steps – where there weren't any decent hiding-places. I decided not to sneak a look round the corner in case he was trying to trick me into showing myself.

And then, suddenly, there was no need to hold my breath and stay frozen. There came the unmistakable clump of Colin's feet pounding up the steps, followed by the

opening and slamming of
the door. And then,
almost immediately after,
the dim bulb was switched
off and I heard the sound of the key
being turned in the lock.

Chapter Three

At first a flush of panic swept through me and my heart pounded madly. I'd suffocate. The rats would get me. I'd starve to death. They'd never find my body and no one would ever know what had happened to me.

I took a deep breath and plucked up enough courage to feel my way over to the foot of the steps. Edging my way across wasn't as easy as I'd imagined it would be. I stubbed my toes, grazed my shin, knocked my elbow and winded myself against a sharp corner – but I eventually got there.

At the foot of the steps I paused for breath. Somewhere behind me, or perhaps it was only in my head, the rat was scrabbling again. I really was feeling nervous about the next bit. The steps were steep,

and narrow, and there was no handrail;
and if you missed your footing and
tumbled over the edge you'd probably
break your head open on the concrete
floor beneath.

The steps seemed to have got even
narrower in the dark. I hesitated for a
moment and then
decided that the
only way up was
on hands and
knees. I was so
scared whenever
my right hand
reached forward
and upwards and
found nothing
solid that I kept
my left shoulder
tightly pressed to
the wall.

When I finally pushed out my hand and touched the bottom of the door, I almost cried with relief. With trembling legs I slowly pulled myself up and wiped my cheeks with the back of my hand. I wasn't going to give Colin the satisfaction of seeing that he'd upset me.

Without much hope I started
to rap lightly on the door. I
was amazed when I heard the
key turn and saw the door open
after just the first few taps. Colin
greeted me with an unconvincing laugh.

"Well done, Rod," he said, clapping me
on the shoulder. "You said you could do
it and you did."

It was then that I spotted Aunt Carrie by the kitchen door, with a tea towel in her hand. Colin's little show had been for her benefit.

"Did you lock Roderick in the cellar?" she said.

"Of course not," said Colin, like the natural liar he is.

"Yes, you did," she said; "I've just seen you unlock the door. Well, no more cellar for you today. That's for sure."

Colin knew better than to protest because he didn't want her telling his dad. I breathed a sigh of relief.

Chapter Four

That night, as Colin and I lay in our beds in the dark, and I was just about to fall asleep, he suddenly whispered, "You very nearly got me into trouble, you did."

That was typical. I could have broken my neck because of him and he says I nearly got *him* into trouble.

"But I didn't," I said, "because I didn't scream and I didn't go moaning to your mum and dad."

"And I suppose you think that makes you tough?" said Colin. I could just imagine the sneer on his face. "Well, let me tell you it doesn't," he went on. "You were only brave because you didn't know about the little man with no face. You won't be so brave next time."

We lay there, silently, in the dark bedroom. He was waiting for me to ask, and I was waiting for him to tell me.

He cracked first. Sort of.

"I suppose you want me to tell you about him?" he said, finally.

"If you want," I said, trying to fake a yawn and suppress the lump in my throat at the same time.

"Well," he said, "if you're sure you can take it. The story is" – and here he dropped his voice to an eerie whisper – "that the cellar is haunted. The legend goes back to the Middle Ages ..."

Now I was pretty certain the Middle Ages came well before Victorian houses, but I didn't interrupt. Despite myself, I wanted to hear the story.

"… when – at various times – several servants were found dead in that cellar."

I licked my lips moist. "They fell down the steps?"

"Worse," said Colin, scarcely able to hide his enjoyment, "*much* worse. They all died of fright; in the dark. Their hair had turned white."

"But that was a long time ago," I said, partly to reassure myself.

"He's still there, though, they say," said Colin. "Only he sleeps all the time now. Except when someone's down there without a light."

There was a short pause. "Don't you want to know why he's called 'the little man with no face'?" he asked.

Of course I wanted to know, desperately.

"Well, you see," he said, without waiting for an answer, "he's got a perfectly smooth, round head – with no hair, or ears, or eyes. If he gets you he grabs hold of you by the wrist with his bony little fingers and runs your hand over his face. It's just like feeling a warm, slightly tacky balloon, except that your fingers sink in a bit …"

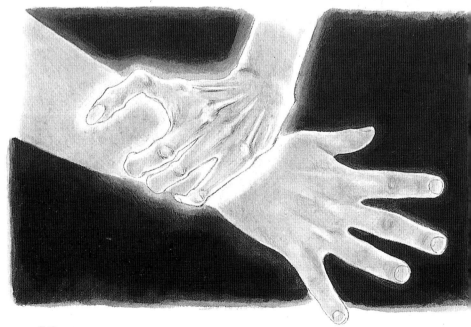

There was probably more, but I was under the bedclothes, unable to speak.

Try as I might, I simply couldn't make myself believe that Colin was inventing it all just to scare me. How I got to sleep I'll never know.

But what a sleep it was. It seemed one long, repeated nightmare with me down in the dark cellar, scrambling on all fours up the wooden steps. Except that the

steps were so soft that my fingers kept sinking in and I couldn't move forward

and a bony hand kept grabbing my ankle
to pull me back and I couldn't make any
sound when I tried to scream.

Chapter Five

The next day Aunt Carrie took us to the
zoo. Luckily Colin didn't bully me too
much because there was plenty to see.
But even though I checked that the key
was turned in the cellar door before I
went up to bed that night, I still had the
same nightmares.

The following day Colin quietly
suggested another game of Cops and
Robbers in the cellar.

"We didn't finish the last game, remember?" he said.

I nodded. "OK by me," I said. I'd managed to seem quite relaxed since he'd tried to scare me and I wasn't going to let him score an easy victory now.

"But no turning the light off," I said. "I could have had a really bad accident when you played that stupid trick. And your dad's going to stop us playing in the cellar if he thinks we're doing anything dangerous."

At the mention of
Uncle Geoff, Colin's
eyes narrowed (well,
narrowed even more than
usual). I could see that he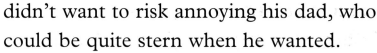
didn't want to risk annoying his dad, who
could be quite stern when he wanted.

"Of course not," he said. "You don't
think I'd want to excite the little man
with no face, do you? What do you take
me for?"

Almost as soon
as I set foot on the
steps (I'd allowed
Colin to go first)
there was a clap of
thunder that made
every bone in my
body rattle. Colin
turned and looked
up at me. "You're

not scared, are you? Because, if you are, we can always play cards, you know." For a second I was surprised at this strange concern for me. And then I noticed his pale cheeks and understood. The thunder, and probably his own ghost story, had rattled him a bit and he wanted an excuse to chicken out.

"I'm fine," I said, keeping my teeth from chattering by a superhuman effort.

Another crash of thunder, and the dim bulb flickered. I winced.

"Well, let's get on with it," Colin snapped, thumping his way down the rest of the steps.

"Right; you hide first," he ordered. "And if you take my advice you'll keep away from the darkest corners. Unless you want to have bony little hands feeling around your ankles and squeezing your arms."

"If he grabs you, just try to keep moving," he went on; "and whatever you do, don't run your hands over his face."

"Thanks. I'll try to remember that," I said, holding on tightly to a work-bench.

"Right. I'll close my eyes and count to ten slowly. Move it!"

I already knew where I was going to hide: behind the hamper near the foot of the steps. That way he couldn't sneak past me without being seen.

"... seven, eight ..."

Crash! The loudest clap of thunder yet. And the light went out.

My heart seemed to stop and I could almost taste my fear. Dizzy with fear and trembling I somehow managed to grope my way to the steps.

With the back of my hand pressed into my mouth to stop myself screaming, I slipped down on to the bottom step. I was shivering all over. But somehow, terrified as I was, I sensed that Colin, at the other end of the cellar, was more terrified still.

"It's all right, Rod," he whispered. "There's nothing to be afraid of. Honestly. All that stuff about the little man with no face – I made it up. Just for a laugh."

40

Some laugh, I thought.

"Look, I don't know where you are," he said. "So if you could find your way over to me we can get up the steps together. That's it …"

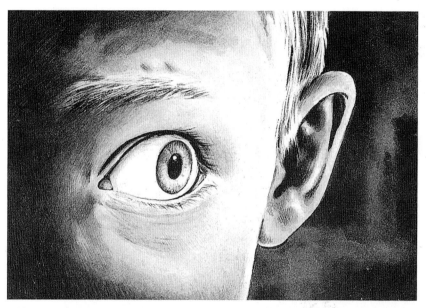

That's it? I hadn't moved. I couldn't. I was sitting, petrified with fear. I wanted to explain to Colin that I was at the steps, but it was just like the nightmare. The words wouldn't come.

"Over here; you're nearly there," he whispered. "Don't be frightened. Just give me your hand, Rod. That's right. And now … Hey, Rod, what are you doing with my hand?"

The scream that followed must have been louder than the thunder outside.

Uncle Geoff certainly heard it in the shed, because it didn't seem any time at all before the door burst open and a flashlight beam swept the cellar.

"You're OK," Uncle Geoff shouted to me as he jumped over me to reach Colin. "Just follow Auntie Carrie's torch beam up the steps. It's nothing. Just the lights fused."

I knew that Colin wasn't dead because I could hear his gasping and sobbing. But when Uncle Geoff brought him up the steps in a fireman's lift, I saw immediately that Colin's hair had turned pure white.

He was fine after he was treated for shock in hospital. They moved to a flat soon after, so there were no more cellar games. I can't say I minded.

DARE TO BE SCARED!

Are you brave enough to try more titles in the Tremors series? They're guaranteed to chill your spine...

Play... if you dare by Ruth Symes
Josie can hardly believe her luck when she finds the computer game at a car boot sale. "Play... if you dare," the game challenges. So she does. Further and further she plays, each level of the game scarier than the last. Then she reaches the last level. "Play... if you dare," repeats the game. But if she does, she could be trapped for ever...

The Claygate Hound by Jan Dean
On the school camp to Claygate, Billy is determined to scare everyone with his terrifying stories of the Claygate Hound, a vicious ghost dog said to lurk nearby. Ryan and Zeb ignore his warnings and explore the woods. They hear a ghostly howl – and run. Has Billy been speaking the truth, or is there a more terrifying reason for what they have heard?

The Curse of the Frozen Loch by Anthony Masters
Why does the ghostly figure skate the loch in the dead of night? And what is wrong with Great-Aunt Fiona? Will and Sarah are determined to solve the mystery and save Fiona. But will they be the next victims of the curse of the frozen loch?

The Ghost of Golfhawk School by Tessa Potter
Martin and Dan love frightening the younger children at school with scary ghost stories. But then Kirsty arrives. Kirsty claims that she can actually see ghosts. Then a mysterious virus sweeps through the school. Martin is still sure she is lying. After all – ghosts don't exist, do they?

All these books and many more can be purchased from your local bookseller. For more information about Tremors, write to: The Sales Department, Hachette Children's Books, 338 Euston Road, London NW1 3BH.